George Henry Calvert

Mirabeau

George Henry Calvert

Mirabeau

ISBN/EAN: 9783337334710

Printed in Europe, USA, Canada, Australia, Japan

Cover: Foto ©Andreas Hilbeck / pixelio.de

More available books at **www.hansebooks.com**

MIRABEAU

AN HISTORICAL DRAMA

BY

GEORGE H. CALVERT

CAMBRIDGE
Printed at the Riverside Press
1873

PERSONS REPRESENTED.

LOUIS XVI., *King of France.*

MARIE ANTOINETTE, *his Queen.*

COUNT MIRABEAU.

COUNT LA MARK.

GENERAL LA FAYETTE.

COUNT MONTMORIN, *one of the King's Ministers.*

MALHERBES.

CECILE.

HENRI.

ABBÉ BIENVILLE.

PRESIDENT OF THE BANK ST. CHARLES.

POET AND TWO MEN OF LETTERS.

TWO STOCK-GAMBLERS.

GUILBERT.

LABORERS.

TWO MEMBERS OF THE ASSEMBLY.

ROBESPIERRE.

MARAT.

THREE PRIESTS.

TWO MONEY-LENDERS, WITH A CLERK.

Citizens, Attendants, etc.

SCENE, — *Paris at the opening of the French Revolution.*

MIRABEAU.

ACT I.

SCENE I.

A Street in a Village, just outside one of the Gates of Paris, at the end of April, 1789. A Holiday. A number of Laborers, Women, and Children.

FIRST LABORER.

WE come from the deeps of the dark ages past :
The loads of our fathers we carry them still :
Still numb˙are our bosoms from tyranny's blast,
And palsied the muscles that do others' will.

SECOND LABORER.

To workers is Time but a weigher of woe :
At night we lie hungry, rise hopeless at morn ;
And all the dear hours are the torturers slow
Of us who are fettered before we are born.

THIRD LABORER.

We sweat and we toil that the barons have feasts:
The work is all ours, and the pay is all theirs:
They rule us and ride us, and make of us beasts,
Whom God made, like them, of his bounty the heirs.

FIRST LABORER.

We're brothers and husbands, we're fathers and sons:
They yoke and they drive us like cattle from pen.
The blood in our hearts shall it creep as in nuns?
Are we not all Frenchmen, and are we not men?

SECOND LABORER.

Then men let us be. We will die or we'll live
Not stifled in sighs, not to tyrants a prey.
Henceforth, then, ourselves to ourselves we will give;
We have but to will, and we're stronger than they.

A scream outside, and in rushes CECILE, *pursued by two lackeys in livery. She escapes among the crowd, and the two lackeys endeavoring to seize her are resisted by the laborers.*

LACKEY.

Base hinds, ragged canaille, how dare you balk us?
Away, chaff! See you not our livery? Know you not
who is behind us?

FIRST LABORER.

Painted swine, servile braggarts, blustering slaves, too well we know you —

LACKEY (*to his fellow*).

François, go call the Marquis.

CECILE (*clinging to* FIRST LABORER).

O save me! save me —

FIRST LABORER.

While there's a pulse in this arm it shall shield you. Frenchmen, her cause is our cause: her wrong cries to our manhood. Pimps of the tyrants are these swaggering flunkeys. Shall we not snatch her from their fangs?

MANY VOICES.

We will: we will!

Enter the MARQUIS, *dressed in the fashion of the day, with a friend similarly dressed.*

MARQUIS.

Rascals, low-born, foul-fed knaves, how dare you thrust your hands between me and my will? Know you not my livery? I am the Marquis of Matignan.

A LABORER.

O, *I* know you.   Because my father would not sell
his child to your lust, you turned him sick out of his
house in winter.

MARQUIS.

Jacques, François, take the girl.

The workmen resist : several of them raise sticks.

MARQUIS (*drawing his sword*).

Rank scum, I'll make a corpse of him that strikes.

Enter MIRABEAU, *with a friend.*

MIRABEAU.

Put up your sword : no place is this for swords.

MARQUIS.

Whence is your right to speak so royally ?
Your mien and dress denote you of our side.

MIRABEAU.

I'm on the side o' the wronged against their wrongers.

MARQUIS.

Big phrases often hide base ends.   Enough,
This your self-thrusting in is insolence :   .
Draw and defend yourself.

MIRABEAU.

       Put up your sword :
The time's too fiery full for private brawls.

MARQUIS.

Who, what are you ? You bear you as you had
Authority. Your name ?

MIRABEAU.

   Count Mirabeau.

LABORERS.

Long live Count Mirabeau, the People's friend !

MARQUIS.

The mob's foul breath is fitting stuff to weave
A title for the noble renegade.

MIRABEAU.

Scorn tow'rds the many, gorged on pride's excess,
With self-applause and arrogant despite,
These are the devils that so have ruled the few
Who rule the land, the People's heart is ·swol'n
With the slow poison of revenge and hate,
And jocund France turned to a wilderness,
Where rages startle Heaven with hungry howl.

MARQUIS.

Is't Heaven or Hell that chooses you, to whet
This hate and brutal greed?   Think you your birth,
Count Mirabeau, befits this factious part?

MIRABEAU.

My manhood is to me more than my name;
My thought's conviction and my heart's full throb
Are nearer me than titled accidents.

MARQUIS.

All that you are, — whatever that may be, —
You owe, Sir Count, to your descent and name.
We'll make you curse the day you turned your back
Upon your order's ranks.

MIRABEAU.

'Twas ever thus.
Chief office of the sacred order is,
To make yourselves bloodhounds to hunt and tear
The People's friends.   And happens it, of these
That one springs from your loins, for him your yelp
Is a continuous scream of thirstiest wrath.
Thus by the fury of Patricians fell,
At Rome, the last of the great Gracchi, Caius,
Who, as he sank, invoked th' avenging gods,

Flinging tow'rds Heaven the dust whence Marius
    sprang, —
Marius, less great that he the warlike Cimbri quelled,
Than that he smote Patrician arrogance.

MARQUIS.

A paltering demagogue and Roman scourge —
Choice models for ambitious Mirabeau.
I leave you, sir, to the high company
Of these applauders.   Apter their ears are
Than mine to listen to seditious wrangle.
We'll meet elsewhere.

              [Exeunt MARQUIS *and his friend.*

MIRABEAU.

            Aye with sedition's brand
Tyrants would blacken every lifted front
That heaves it up, through weak debasement's gloom,
Struggling for light towards the great Sun of Justice.
'Twixt man and man Justice is the prime need:
Its cordial light, if from the many shut,
Is lessened for the whole : nay, if denied
Even to a few, all of its beams are dimmed.
In France so dim is't now, men are a prey
The many to the few, and these, the few,
To monsters warped, as fatal to themselves
As to the nation's health they feed upon,

Grown rank through fat immunities perverse,
Their privileges 'gainst strong nature strained,
Their joys ensteeped in mourners' tears, their life
A sore, that from the worker's toil-spent veins
All the sweet humors sucks and turns to poison,
That throws its tainture on the general blood.

GUILBERT.

Your words put new resolves into my brain.
There's nothing brave men will. not greatly dare
When led by greatness.   These new forceful times
Need a high soul to master and conduct them.

MIRABEAU.

So foaming deep is the fresh, manful life
That surges in men's hearts, 'twill need the might
Of many earnest souls to temper it.

FIRST LABORER.

From the States-General, Count, may we not hope?
O ! do not say we may not.   'Tis a joy,
A new, uplifting joy, for us to hope :
We never hoped before.

MIRABEAU.

            Hug your new guest :
Press to your hearts with warmest welcome's cheer

The late-come angel, hope.   'Tis a great right '
You have resumed, the greatest, dearest right
Of the blest issue it shall propagate.
Nurse it, clasp it with all your being's strength.
What loads of wrong, what depths of untold woe
Unmasks this dreadful lack of daily hope,
Manhood's vast might and deep security.
By the regaining of this long-lost gift
Half freed you are already.   Breath from Heaven
Hath blown this blessing to your stifled hearts.

FIRST LABORER.

Stifled we are, panting for air to live by.
But on a sudden seems now oped above
A wider space that leaves more room to breathe.

MIRABEAU.

Periods there are when all mysteriously,
Yet palpably, come influxes that float,
Upon their viewless, providential tides,
Stranded humanity.   And this is one
Of those high epochs.   Slow is liberty
To be possessed: as coy she is as pure,
And will be wooed by none but cleansèd hearts.
Of her great countenance we've caught a glimpse
By Heaven's light, prophetic in our souls ;
And now our will, our might, our life we give

To compass her and hold her.   Not for us
Shall be th' enjoyment: to our children's heirs
In the far time shall come fruition full.
They shall revere and thank us that we were
Heralds and martyrs for the glorious realm
Of Law and Liberty, where they shall bide.

[Exeunt MIRABEAU and friend.

CECILE.

(*As* MIRABEAU *was speaking she had come close to him, and listened
intently.*)

From his great eyes and words what a soul speaks !
Would he were King !   Then might we hope indeed.
My friends, — for such you've proved yourselves to
        me, —
Think not that I mean treason ; but the flood
Of this man's speech lifts me above myself.

FIRST LABORER.

Me, too : I'm twice the man I was.   With him
I'll wade through fire and death.   Did he not speak
Of martyrs, and that we shall not enjoy
The freedom that is surely coming ? — Hush !

SCENE II.

The Same.

To them enter a Poet *and two* Men of Letters.

POET.

Good friends, Heaven favors you to-day with warmth.

SECOND LABORER.

Aye, sir, without the Sun a holiday
Were half a gift to us.

POET.

All of your days
Will be hereafter gifts more generous
Than now your happiest restful holiday.

SECOND LABORER.

On what the Estates will do count you so much?

POET.

The Estates will be the nimble instruments
Of public will.   Henceforth the general wish
Shall be the binding law.   Slow, faithful Time,
The patient mother, long hath groaned in travail
With a great birth, begot by manful thought.

Soon she shall bless the world with this new babe,
The greatest she has borne, — freedom for all.

SECOND LABORER.

Shall we all be free? Shall we all be free? No
more task-masters, no more taxes, no more tithes?

THIRD LABORER.

Shall we grind our own corn, and press our own
grapes? Shall all our work be for ourselves, none for
the baron, none for the priest?

FOURTH LABORER.

Shall we work when we please and play when we
please, and shall we be free not to work?

POET.

No man is free not to work. Freedom is
Work's strongest child, and owes his sire a debt
Which he can only pay in kind; and so,
The freer a man is, so much more he'll need,
Nay, love to work. Your mind doth live by work,
And feeds you with its work; but poorly yet,
Because you are enslaved. What now you do,
Obedient vassals, coarsely and with pain,
Rudely, unwillingly, you'll do with joy,

When all your shackles you have shaken off.
Pigmies you now are, dwarfs, not half yourselves.
When thought and speech and will and act are free,
Giants you'll be, your work creative play,
Delighting freemen and yourselves ; your thoughts
Glib messengers, scaling the pilèd air
To talk with stars, girdling the rapid earth
Daily to prompt with worthy novelties
Th' audacious, gladful, forward, soaring mind,
Upswung by work to ever higher planes.

CECILE.

'Tis not a poet's dream : I feel 'tis true.

FIRST MAN OF LETTERS.

Deep truth it is, and yet a poet's dream.
Sprung joyful from the soul's untainted core,
The poet's dream is often truthfuller
Than wakeful'st word or act of daily men ;
For the true poet's heart plies its warm pulse
Nearer the central soul's creative throb.

POET.

My friends, I would not flatter you to launch
Unballasted hopes upon the stormy sea
Whose minatory moan even now we hear.
Things the most costly are of slowest growth.

Slowest of all, because most choice of all,
Is freedom, the consummate gain of life,
Gold-harvest sure of sweet self-betterment,
Dearest and deepest of life's conquests slow,
Hoarding them all within its jeweled crown.
From thoughtless dwarfishness we cannot grow
To full man's stature in a single year,
Nor in a score, nay, nor a century.

SECOND MAN OF LETTERS.

But that we have the room to grow, we must
Strike from our limbs at once the sullen chains
That bind us to the tasks of idlers' setting.
As well be mouldering captives of the Turk:
Worse than scorned pirates of Algiers are these
Our home-bred masters.   You are men, strong, brave.
These dukes and counts and barons, and these
        priests,
God made them no more men than he made you.
Rouse ye ! wake up your slumbering manhood's
        might.
Make these proud priests, these lofty lords, to know,
You are their equals.   Men are men, and more
They cannot be.   These would be more than you:
And so they are, because you let them be.
Your weakness is their strength : they have none
        else.

Take this to heart : bethink you what your are :
Then be what you have never been — yourselves,
Your manly selves.

　　　　　　　　[*Exeunt* POET *and* MEN OF LETTERS.

FIRST LABORER.

　　　　　'Tis true, 'tis true, 'tis true :
All that he says is true : we've been asleep.

SECOND LABORER.

But now we're wide awake.　Let's be ourselves.

THIRD LABORER.

Let's be our manly selves.　We know our strength.

GUILBERT.

From my old eyes disabling bandages
Have fall'n this many a year.　We are not babes.
Do grown men need child's nursing?　Look at them,
Those priests.　Their black dress is a twofold lie ;
First, a pretension, then a cloak ; a sign,
They've made men think it is, of ghostly holiness ;
And so, we have not seen it is a cloak,
Behind the which, shut from intrusion's glance,
They boldly play their game for power and pelf.

CECILE.

Kind friends, brave friends, I've found two stalwart
    neighbors
Who'll be companions on my way.   Farewell.

[Exit with two.

SCENE III.

As before: then enter three PRIESTS.

FIRST PRIEST (*to* SECOND LABORER).

Alphonse, my wayward son, where have you been
These many months?   Have you forgotten me,
And what I have to give?

GUILBERT.

              What can you give?
Words, words ; and hitherto we've been the fools, —
And you have done your best to keep us fools, —
To take these words, your hollow words, for things.
'Tis only soul can into words put power.
None but a good man's speech breathes healing
    breath.
What are your lives that you can help us live?

FIRST PRIEST.

Put a fool's cap upon his brazen head,
That all may know his right to speak.   Your tongue
The Devil hath seized, to make a fool seem wise.
Take down his name : I would know more of him.

SECOND PRIEST (*taking out his tablets*).

Sirrah, your name and home.

THIRD LABORER (*to* SECOND PRIEST).

     I'll give you both —
Of one you should know something of. Jeannette !
Be not afraid or shamed.

     [JEANNETTE *comes forward.*

   The shame is his.

THIRD PRIEST (*older than the other two*).

Out on these loose-tongued, graceless, saucy knaves !
They must be looked to. Worse and worse they grow.
Come, let us on.

     [*Exeunt* PRIESTS.

GUILBERT.

    And worse and worse, bad priest,
They still would grow under your backward pull ;
'Tis you have lured them to this ruin's pass ;
Sleek pharisees, fat-feeding dieters,
Jobbers in souls, cheats who for gold sell prayers —
Not prayers, the brazen counterfeit of prayers.
Thieves of men's pith, ye steal from us our best,
Our deeper life, and put it in your bellies.
But now rewakened is the giant, manhood,
That slept so long. A new dawn breaks, and by
Its loving beams we read a mighty word,

That rises beckoning from our quickened deeps,
Where the great things it stands for lie unclaimed ;
Rights, that's the magic word.   At last we feel
That we have rights, and, feeling so, we know
That whoso hold them from us are usurpers.
Light is strength, and this timid dawn will mount
To midday breadth and valor.   Then shall we,
Strong in our practiced manhood, shake to naught
All usurpations, all these crosses, racks,
Man's gross devices, that prohibit us,
Cramping, perverting, robbing our best powers,
Powers God-given.   Chief of these hard tyrannies
Is Priesthood, sucking at our very souls.

SCENE IV.

As before.   Enter two Money-Lenders, *with their*
Clerk.

Here are more robbers, only that they prowl
In other paths.   What seek ye here, ye leeches ?
In these pale carcasses there is no blood.

FIRST MONEY-LENDER.

What madman has been loosed upon the street
To grin at passers by ?

GUILBERT.

You know me not,
Sir Harpagon ?   Your victims are so many,
One memory cannot hold them all.

SECOND MONEY-LENDER.

Rash churl,
Tether your tongue, and shut behind your teeth
Your tartness, lest it bring about your ears
Something rougher than words.   What's the foul trade
That blackens you to such crude jealousy?

GUILBERT.

Fouler than yours, Sir Grip, it could not be :
I'd smell too rank for contact with my fellows.

SECOND MONEY-LENDER *offers to strike him and is prevented by* FIRST.

FIRST MONEY-LENDER.

Nay — nay : Guilbert and I are early friends.
Soft words go far with him.   Why should not we
Ply our trade, too, as you ply yours, good Guilbert?
Ours is a necessary trade.   Yourself,
In foregone years, by it were saved from ruin.

GUILBERT.

Saved with the stinging loss, in two short months,
Of half my life-earned gains.   A necessary trade !

Which prospers most when men are most in want.
When others droop in grief your joy is ripest.
When toil-bent backs are tottering with their loads,
You come all smiles, and kindly offer, aye,
You kindly offer them, with bows, to add
Another measure to their sleepless burthen,
Your gain's degree, and thence your gladness' range,
Scored by the depth of their dejectedness.

SECOND MONEY-LENDER.

Away ! We'll hear no more such ribaldry.

GUILBERT.

You shall hear more : you shall. The time is come
When voices sound were never heard before,
Voices that break the silences of ages ;
And could they speak with the due trumpet-blast
They'd crack the drums of your cold, guilty ears,
That you to each day's healing music were
As deaf, as you have been to the long cries
Of orphans starved, of helpless, hopeless fathers,
Of mothers moaning — of that motley throng,
The prey of ruthless usury.

FIRST MONEY-LENDER (*trying to move away*).
                                        No more :

I'll hear no more.

GUILBERT.

You shall hear more ; and more.
Look at this silver piece: your know it well,
Too well ; and yet you know it not.   You know
It is a Spanish coin, sure messenger
Around the globe, bidding the costliest wares,
Wherever shelved, to flit at its arrival.
You know 'tis master of all outward things ;
That thence, when counted into coffers deep.
It links to you the longing looks of men,
And thus brings power, consideration's gloss,
And every worldling's homage.   For all this,
You know it not.   You know its skin, its face ,
It hath a heart, a soul : it stands for work,
Many, many long hours of toil, sad toil,
Compressed into this petty circle's bound.
A distillation is it from the sweat
Of straining manhood, precious diamond drop
Plucked from the brain of labor ; and 'tis thus
A sacred thing.   Who wastes it, is a fool
Or felon ; who misuses it, a knave.
O could you but behold it with new eyes !
Looking with your old worn ones, dim with greed,
'Twere scarce a miracle if, as you gaze,
Its pallid face should ooze big ruddy tears ;
For every atom of its costly ore
Was kneaded warm with blood from brothers' veins,
From faint, deserted brothers.

FIRST AND SECOND MONEY-LENDERS (*rushing away*)

Enough, enough.

[*Exeunt.*

CLERK.

I'll eat their bread no more.   Rather than that
I'll delve upon the highway, sweep the sewers.
'Tis but a little while I've dwelt with them.
I will not spend the earnings of such service.
Here, take it.

Throws handfuls of coin to the crowd, then exit.

SCENE V.

Cecile's Apartment.

CECILE (*alone*).

Is life a scramble for the needs of life?
No more than that?   And in this scramble's shock
Often to lose the needs and very self?
It seems so in this demoniac town,
Where passions now are loosed before were chained,
Were watched so close they dared not even growl.
A thousand lions in a wilderness,
Their manes aglow, preluding for a war,
More ruthless could not roar defiantly.
My woman's heart 'twould daunt, were I not roused
By faith, the faith my mother from her breast

Poured into mine, so clear, so steadily, —
Earth's sharpest scourges are not worth a fear :
The higher self, the soul, th' immortal me,
Lives safe, licensed 'gainst harm save from within.
Fears for myself I've few ; but for my Henri !
Pitfalls and traps and lures sprout here as thick
As they were nature's free unprompted crop.
But he is quick of sight and sure of heart.

Enter HENRI.

HENRI.

O my dear Cecile, thou art well ?

CECILE.

                         Well, Henri ?
This morning thou wast here.   There is no plague
In Paris, in the air no epidemic
Raining a brisk infection on the blood ?

HENRI.

'Tis worse than that : infected is the blood
With malice, greed, and ulcerated wraths.
Men look like gnashing demons loosed from jail,
That jail a sour, litigious, raveled hell,
Where they have learnt naught but perversity.

CECILE.

These lessons touch us not ; nor must thou strive
With thy pure oil to smooth this noisome rage.
I would we were all back in still Toulouse.

HENRI.

Not I, not I. This vast combustion's shout
Makes my veins tingle with a salter blood.
The torrent must be stayed, or else we sweep
Headlong to brutal lawlessness. There's much,
Aye, everything to do. Of what we've done
In six red-heated moons, the most is misdone.
We're all too hot for wisdom.

CECILE.

                        Mirabeau,
What seems he now to thee ?

HENRI.

                        I cannot say.
He is too big for present apprehension.
With Time's still ripening juices mind must swell,
To weigh the thunderbolts of a new Jove,
Hurled fiery from the darkening depths of France.
Would we could trust him.   Then he were a hope,
Would streak the black expanse of thickening gloom
As moonlit path an angered ocean's frown.

CECILE.

Dear Henri, trust a woman's intuition.
My meeting him, some months gone by, thou know'st,
When he helped rescue me from ruffians.   There,
As I gazed gratefully and heard him speak,
My soul grew momently more kin to his.

HENRI.

The man doth fascinate whoever falls
Within th' encounter of his eye or voice.

CECILE.

In this man's soul are depths unfathomed yet.
Might wed to tenderness makes that eye's power.

HENRI.

He'll speak to-day, and I must to my seat.
Dear Cecile, now I leave thee.   Nay, not so.
Where'er I am or go, thou'rt with me there,
A circumfusèd atmosphere of joy,
Refreshing balsam to my stalest thought,
A consolation's balm to every wound,
A ceaseless presence, hallowing my life.
Cecile, the year is nearly ended, dearest:
Let now thy sweetest wishes mate with mine,
That ere the new one I may call thee wife.

CECILE.

Best Henri, be it so.   Nearer to me
Thou then wilt be: dearer thou canst not be.
In thee I am so blest, I sometimes fear
Increase of happiness will fill my cup
To overflowing, and so spill the whole.

HENRI.

Why wilt thou let dark thoughts attaint thy brain?
Be aye thy luminous self.   Adieu, adieu.

Enter the ABBÉ BIENVILLE.

ABBÉ.

Henri! not in your seat to-day?   .

HENRI.

                              What's up?

ABBÉ.

Mirabeau, flashing and thundering.

HENRI.

                              Adieu.
                                        [*Exit.*
ABBÉ.

I will not hear, for I can't answer him.

CECILE.

And who can answer him? Pigmies ye all,
Were he a common man.   But ye are men
Of common stature, — some above the mean, —
And he's a giant.   Not to cope with him
Detracts from no man's manhood.   But to learn,
By listening to him, that's a privilege
This age o'ertops all others in.

ABBÉ.

Cecile,   ·

Sweet cousin, tell me, why do women all
Commend, extol, adore this Mirabeau?

CECILE.

Women's brains teem with stout ideal men :
These help to polish them and quicken them.
When of these secret images of love
One leaps forth bodied to their senses' reach,
A speaking, acting personality,
A moving might moulded beyond their visions, —
Shaped, disciplined, and tutored by his greatness,
Exalted by his strange, excessive height,
Their dreams come more than true, — of this new
        man
They're proud with something of warm parents' pride,
And loving, lifting him, they lift themselves.

3

ABBÉ.

My answer's channel is much straighter. Women
Love him, because of his great love for women.

CECILE.

Men, women, children, all that lives he loves.
His o'erabounding, busy love it is
That adds the most to make him what he shows.

ABBÉ.

Does woman always love where she is loved?

CECILE.

The heart is not so blunt mechanical
That it should instant throb to outward touch.
A woman who is woman aptest is
To ope the virgin petals of her love
Where a true warmth woos for their fragrancy;
And even when she cannot interchange
Will with a sigh distill some tenderness.

ABBÉ.

Cecile, O Cecile, hast thou not long seen
How I do love thee!

CECILE.

       Love! Love me! Etienne!

ABBÉ.

For years, long years.   I dared not speak before.

CECILE.

How dar'st thou now ?

ABBÉ.

                Cecile, look not so black
Upon me.

CECILE.

        Black !   Were my looks lightning, and
Could shatter thee, I'd let them loose.   Bad priest,
Worse man : for the priest's badness is a brat
Of rankness in the man : Belial's spawn !

ABBÉ.

Hear me, O hear me —

CECILE.

                Silence !   Think thee blest
If e'er again thou art allowed to speak
With tongue so foul to me, so false to God.

ABBÉ.

Thou must, thou shalt hear me.   O God !. O God !

CECILE.

Blaspheme not : rank are thy best thoughts. God
　　hears not
A voice from such a sink. Thou'st lost thy right
To name Him. Purge thee first with penances,
Purgations, deep atonements.

ABBÉ.

　　　　　　　O I will,
I will. Forgive me, O forgive me. Lay
What penances thou wilt : I'll bear them all,
Bear them, and think them happiness.

CECILE.

　　　　　　Forgive thee !
Canst thou forgive thyself?

ABBÉ.

　　　　　Let me begin
With thy forgiveness. That will give me strength
More than all else. I'm guilty, O, how guilty !
I feel it now : let me not feel't too deeply.

CECILE.

I see thy heart is touched. Étienne, I do
Forgive thee.

ABBÉ.

Angel !

CECILE.

What forgiveness carries,
That, too, thou hast, my fellow-feeling.

ABBÉ.

Sister !

CECILE.

Thou lost thy mother when thou wast a babe,
And never found'st another.   O 'tis hard
To thrive without some mother ; and for thee,
Thy womanly nature needed most this cordial.
Étienne, I'll be a mother to thee.   'Tis
A holy function each of us can ply
To be a mother to the motherless.

ABBÉ.

O, thou canst save me, canst absolve me here.

[*Kneels.*

CECILE.

God only can absolve thee ; even He
Only through thine own heart.   When thou shalt feel
The spotless, the divine, in vivid presence ;
When sparkling, self-found springs shall so have
    cleansed

Thy inmost, that thy fullest wishes' stream
Flows outward from thyself, thou then art ripe
For absolution ; then art thou absolved,
Thou'rt self-absolved.   No man, none, can absolve
Another than himself. — Leave me now.

[*Exit* Abbé.

The Curtain falls.

ACT II.

SCENE I.

Mirabeau's Apartment.

MIRABEAU (*alone*).

ONE year! Not yet a year! And what a year!
The sky, the earth, the air, all are aglow
With a strange heat, solstitial circumambience,
Breathed burning from the kindled souls of men,
Wherein thoughts bold and bolder — like mad flames
From roof to roof — leap wild from head to head,
Folding the whole mazed mass in conflagration.
Chaos come back it seems — for awhile is.
From sunless caves of ignorance upswarming,
From lonely towers of privilege outdriven,
Dazzled, half-blinded now are men by light,
The new light gushing from impassioned mind,
Mind loosed upon damned despotism's long dusk,
And doomed so sharp to blister it with flame,
It shall flee like a murderous robber's race
From swift-pursuing dawn's detective flash.
But now how black and torrid glares all France!

A weltering, ghastly furnace of red passion,
Where maddened greed scowls at his neighbor greed,
And drunken anger throws away the scabbard.
A frothy lawlessness, Hell's carnival ! —
There is no lawlessness.   Great Law, supreme,
Unsleeping, plies in peerless majesty
Behind this billowy mist, gazing at it
As loving father on his children's gambols.

Enter a SERVANT.

SERVANT.

Two gentlemen ask, sir, an interview.

[*Gives their cards.*

MIRABEAU.

Admit them.

[*Exit* SERVANT.

   Two stock-gamblers, men of brass,
Who gild themselves with gold and call it gain.

Enter two STOCK-GAMBLERS.

FIRST STOCK-GAMBLER.

But a few moments of your crowded time
We crave, Count Mirabeau.   As enemies
We are not come, though you would make us such.
Friends we would be with men preponderant.

MIRABEAU.

The sharpest utterance of a public man
Against abuses, carries in its tooth
No personal venom for the practicers.
Your trade is hurtful to the general weal.

FIRST STOCK-GAMBLER.

We do but buy and sell as others do.

MIRABEAU.

So does the croupier at the gaming-table ;
But his, like your deeds, turn on wheels of chance,
Wheels that ne'er add a value to their load.
Your toil is barren : if 'twere only that.
The limping beggar draws from me a coin,
By him unearned ; but he does me a good,
It may be, in that he starts in my breast
A tear which more than pays the petty coin.
But you start currents of unhealthy lusts,
And, while I'm giddied by their rushing flood,
You filch my pockets to o'erfill your own.

SECOND STOCK-GAMBLER.

Your skill with words, Sir Count, all the world knows.
We come for business.   You have injured us
By pamphlets.   We shall gain by paying you,

To cease these pamphlets, fifty louis monthly.
Here's for the first.   Each month 'twill be renewed.

FIRST STOCK-GAMBLER.

And good words for us will redouble it.
You hesitate?

[MIRABEAU *walks away.*

MIRABEAU.

Not so: doubting I was
Whether I should let loose my anger's gust.
But wherefore?   Insult was not in your thought.
'Tis too well known I have voracious wants;
Wants bred of vices, poisonous stem of wants.
But these reach not my manhood, my soul's life.
Could I, for my quick sensual joyment's dance,
Barter my faith, my public duty's sense,
Barter myself against my appetites,
I should go crouching through the scornful streets,
And were not Mirabeau, who carries him,
And has a right to carry him, as straight
As does the loftiest he that treads the earth.
Gentlemen, you have children?

FIRST STOCK-GAMBLER.

Aye, we have.

MIRABEAU.

For the full revenues of teeming France
You would not sell a child ?

FIRST STOCK-GAMBLER.

Not for all France.

[*The* SECOND STOCK-GAMBLER *walks away.*

MIRABEAU.

I have no children of my body's birth.
No great-grandchild will boast that in his veins
Bounds the hot blood of Mirabeau.   A boast,
Aye, a big boast it were, when the time comes,
And come it will, that calumny and hate,
With all their swarthy, fiendish, hump-backed brood,
Or shall have died outright, strangled by truth,
Or hid them in unaired imaginations.   .
But I have offspring of my mind, my soul,
Beliefs, convictions, fervent, stout, beloved,
Convictions of my dues to France, to men ;
And these I would not sell for all the wealth
Arithmetic can count or fancy forge.

FIRST STOCK-GAMBLER.

I pray you, sir, forgive us a mistake.
This interview I set much value on.

SECOND STOCK-GAMBLER (*aside*).

No man but has his price.   Men are big fools ;
But biggest have the sense to sell themselves.
Our purse lacks weight to knock this Titan down.

[*Exeunt* STOCK-GAMBLERS.

MIRABEAU.

How my past acts palsy my present power !
O God ! What tyrants men are o'er themselves !
Closest enchainment, closer than wove mail,
Is man's one life.   Between its sequent acts
You cannot thrust even a thought's fine edge,
To part them from their stern dependency,
But each will stream into the younger one,
A procreative, necessary soul.
Once launched, a man grows to be his own maker :
A function how divine, but how appalling !

Enter a SERVANT *and gives him a card.*

Is he below ?

SERVANT.

Aye, sir, he is.

MIRABEAU.

Admit him.

[*Exit* SERVANT

Another purchaser.   This is too much.
But why be angry ?   If I mask myself,
How can men know me ?

Enter the PRESIDENT *of the St. Charles Bank.*

PRESIDENT.
>   Sir — Count Mirabeau —

MIRABEAU.

Well, sir, what is your business ?   Pray, be brief.

PRESIDENT.

The President of the wealthy bank, St. Charles —

MIRABEAU.

Go on.   What would the President of this bank ?

PRESIDENT.

I've learnt — I've learnt, sir, from your publisher,
You have a book in press, to be soon issued,
A book against our bank.

MIRABEAU.
>   That's true.

PRESIDENT.
>   This book
Will be for sale when published ?

MIRABEAU.
>   Surely 'twill.
Books are thus published that they may be sold.

PRESIDENT.

Could this one not be bought before 'tis published ?

MIRABEAU.

If you, sir, are so eager for its freight,
I'll write a line at which my publisher
Will sell to you a copy in advance.

PRESIDENT.

I'd like to buy all of it in advance ;
And for the whole will give five hundred louis.

MIRABEAU.

Five thousand would not buy it.

PRESIDENT (*astonished*).
                         Is that so ?

MIRABEAU.

'Tis so.   Debts, debts I have ; aye, many debts ;
And passions, habits, vices, that make debts ;
And money I must have ; aye, sir, I must.
And yet, nor you nor all the golden heaps
In all the bloated banks of Christendom
Can buy a piece of me.

PRESIDENT.

Count Mirabeau,
Forgive me, sir, forgive me.   At a distance,
I've looked and wondered at, admired and feared
Count Mirabeau ; and now that I've come near him
I more admire, to admiration adding
Deepest respect and, let me say it, love.

MIRABEAU.

Good sir, abuse, hate, calumny, and sneer,
To these, — chafing as 'tis to be misknown, —
I'm hardened ; but to love, to soft, warm words,
I melt as would a woman.   Take my hand.
This day you make one of my happy days ;
You bring me a new friend.   Say to the world,
Mirabeau is not what it takes him for :
It doth misjudge me, cruelly misjudge me.
But I have given it cause, yea, too much cause.
Had I been what I might have been !   Ha — then —
How vain to send good wishes to the past.

> [*As* MIRABEAU *walks away self-communing, the* PRESIDENT
> *withdraws with signs of admiration and sympathy.*

Who is all that he might have been?   No man
But meddling circumstance, or late or early,
Hath wrenched from straightest path: rude circum-
    stance,
That thwarts or warps our aim.   What then are we?

Tools or the workmen, subjects or the King?—
Base whining is 't to rail at fortune's frowns.
Not what I might have been, but what I am,
What might be, that's my matter.   All that's done
Is done by clean impulsion from within.
I, who can sway this fierce democracy,
Can I not rule myself?

Enter LA MARK.

Count de La Mark!
A moment since there stood another there!

LA MARK.

I met him as I entered.

MIRABEAU.

A new friend,
A warm one.

LA MARK.

Shall I not be jealous of him?

MIRABEAU.

Thou jealous!   Thou, a friend, the like of whom
Man never had!

LA MARK.

And was there ever man
So lifted up, so blest, so glorified,
As I have been by this my love for thee ?

MIRABEAU.

O thou didst snatch me from despair's black brink.
When by the weights I've let the past heap on me
I was about to sink, thou heldst me up.

LA MARK.

'Twas my good fortune to be near thee then.
But what was that to what thou'st done for me !
Thou hast outswelled my being, given me a share
In thy vast thoughts ; a partner in thy wealth,
The wealth as yet untold, of thy great heart,
Thou'st made me.   All my other prides are steeped,
Aye, swallowed up in this, that I can serve thee.
My name posterity will lift thus stamped, —
" Count de La Mark, the friend of Mirabeau."
Now wilt thou let thy friend be frank with thee ?

MIRABEAU.

Franker I am than most men with myself ;
And thou, my better self, shalt be still franker.

4

LA MARK.

Of the rich banker who was here just now
I'm jealous.   He's a noble, generous man.

MIRABEAU.

The lion breaks from his strong keeper's hold —
But I'll not tear thee ; nor have I this time
Broke from my cage.   I've promised thee that none
Shall lend me save thyself, — and this I'll keep.
Would I could keep my self-given promises.
Passion o'erswells me so, at times so packs
My veins with fire, it seems I should go mad,
Or burst my brain.   Thy sober pulse, dear Count,
Ne'er shook thee with an inward tempest's rush.
Were it not thine I could begrudge this quiet.

LA MARK.

Wanting thy racy ferment in the blood,
With thunder thou hadst never awed th' Assembly.

MIRABEAU.

His lightning sometimes sears the thunderer.
The keenest joy hath too the sharpest sting.
Life at white heat burns while it blesses you.
Now, shall I call thee blest or curst in this,
That woman moveth not thy depths, that thou
Art proof against love's terrible attractions ?

LA MARK.

I do not let them master me.   But thee
They overpower, ravish, and then rob.

MIRABEAU.

These are brave metaphors ; but will they bear
Translation into fact?   Life must have vent :
Hot life, quick vent : strong life, rich satisfaction.
What is my life, what is my freedom, if
My stream's warm rush be thwarted, checked, and
        dammed?

LA MARK.

Dear Count, our life is mortised in conditions.
Countless are dependencies, large or fine.
There's one condition which, like very soul,
Clings to each act that will be true and good
And have a clean success : it must harm none.
Give life its fullest head : do and be doing,
Warmly and strongly : but, in hottest deed
Do injury to none, neither to thee
Nor to thy neighbor.   Then, as safe thou art
As strong, and each act a beneficence.
By this condition is thy freedom gauged. —
'Tis now my hour when I must to the King.

MIRABEAU.

O were he but a King, a King in soul !

King Log, swell-buffeted, a spongy log,
He drifts upon the ridge of whirlpool's coil,
Dull to the swiftly-narrowing gurge's grip.
Weak men hark aye to lack-wit's mad advice:
Clean echo to their feebleness is flattery.
Deaf imbecility, in self-defense,
Counsel repels which were its sole defense:
Upon its stagnant nerve melodious wisdom
Is voice of nightingale in owlet's ear.
And La Fayette, who cannot know himself;
And me he will not know. — Say to the King —
But why force food on indigestion's maw?

LA MARK.

At times I make him hear.

MIRABEAU.

Speak to the Queen:
She is the only man they have.

LA MARK.

Adieu.

MIRABEAU.

Adieu.
[*Exit* LA MARK.

The Scene closes.

SCENE II.

A room in the Tuileries.

MARIE ANTOINETTE (*alone*).

A Royal House divided 'gainst itself,
How can it stand?   O jealousy! what broods
Of envies and of hates gather beneath
The withering tremor of thy wing.   Our house
Is split to fragments, and of the rent limbs
Each thinks himself the stronger by himself,
Now when the tree needs the compacted pith
Of each with all to root it for the storm
Which threats the very trunk of royalty.
There's one who feeds the storm's voraciousness,
The traitor!   Worst of traitors, royal traitor!
What earthly doom awaits his infamy?
But are dooms final on our little earth?
And must not life, for ripe completion's crown,
Stretch unallayed into the bright beyond?
Or bright or dim, as on it shall be cast
Or light or darkness by each human self.
Self-woven are the crowns we then shall wear, —
Be they of beams, of flowers, or stinging thorns, —
Wove by the shuttle of our earthly wills.
But what speak I of dooms, who am myself

The taunted plaything of a brutish mob.
A King and Queen imprisoned in their palace!
Down, down! proud spirit of my mother, down!
Thou art French now, poor Marie Antoinette!
And thou must take what the French offer thee.

Enter the KING.

Sire, what's the last bad news?

KING.

                    Wilt thou ne'er cease
To see but blackest clouds?

QUEEN.

                    I see what's there, —
Clouds black, and blacker.   Show me a hope:
Let but a rainbow, aye, the faintest bloom,
Light up these thickening curtains of despair —
O I will hug the vision to my breast
As though it were a reblown girlish joy.
None will appear: there is no sovereign Sun. —
The Church, — our necessary wheel, — they've broken
Grasping its rich domains with one rude clutch;
And ere they've done gorging them on their prey
They aim destruction at the Provinces.

KING.

Our chief of foes, the Duke, I've banished.

QUEEN.

Aye,

That's well ; but he will plot where'er he be.
'Tis long since I have seen our courteous jailer.

KING.

Our jailer ! Whom mean you?   Not La Fayette ?

QUEEN.

The same : our jailer and our master.   Aye,
Our master.   Keeps he not us both enjailed ?
And dared he, he would try a guiltier deed.

KING.

You wrong him, harshly wrong him.   Did he not
At Versailles save you ?

QUEEN.

Yea, he did, he did :

I do believe he did.   I am unjust.
I lose me in the darkness that enfolds me.
Even the happy are not always just ;
How can the wretched be so?

KING.

Mirabeau,

Tow'rds him, too, thou'rt unjust.

QUEEN.

How can I be ?
Can words paint him too dark, or deeds smite him
Too roughly.   Would that he and La Fayette
Were with the Duke, away.

KING.

Then were we ruined.

QUEEN.

We can be ruined only by ourselves.
No man or men can touch us harmfully,
Be we ourselves, ourselves, our regal selves.

Enter MONTMORIN *and* MALHERBES.

O Montmorin, and good Malherbes, dear friends ;
You are our friends ; you will not, too, desert us ?

MONTMORIN.

Not while I've life, or arm, or voice, or will.

KING.

The Queen is much disturbed to-day.

MONTMORIN.

We breathe
Such atmospheres of change, nor thought nor heart

Can keep its poise from day to day.   By blasts
As from a charnel-house our life is bent.
Paris, all France, is one huge sepulchre,
Wherein is hurled, pell-mell, no rite observed,
All that is best, most sacred, most endeared.

QUEEN.

And we meekly attend as helpless mourners.
We shall be thrown alive into this pit.
Gentlemen, something, something must be done.
We're hastening down ; this fall, where will it stop ?
This unresisted, silent, swift descent,
This mountain land-slide to its valley's base,
Shaking the night with one stupendous crash,
Where can it stop but in the depths unseen ?
Shall we surrender, even ere we're summoned ?
The nation waits for us : it cries for action,
Action.   There is no virtue without vigor.
We lack not friends : they droop because we droop.
Scores of brave friends, within th' Assembly's self,
For guidance look to us ; and we are nerveless,
Dumb, motionless as the dull, pinioned ox
Who awaits the butcher's blow.   O for a man !

MONTMORIN.

Madame, 'tis of a man I've come to speak,
If that your Majesty will listen to me.

QUEEN.

With my whole being will I, and wish I had
An hundred ears.

MONTMORIN.

The needed man is one
With sight so visionary true, he can
Forecast events, and thus meet them ahead,
Baffling them ere they show their hideous bulk.
For this, within his own tumultuous bosom
Carry he must the seed of great upheavals,
Have passions, sympathies, warm, active, broad,
That he the surging multitude's hot heart
May hold and sway ; a man of power, with lights
To lead his power.

Enter LA MARK.

QUEEN.

Of such colossal mould
I know but one, and he our foremost foe.

MONTMORIN.

Madame, Count Mirabeau hath seemed your foe :
He is a royalist and gentleman.
That he's a tribune, with a voice that quells
Or rouses, at his will, — a strange, new voice
Burning with marrowy life, — this we can make,

If we're expedient, servant to our cause.
The People love him, not for his opinions :
These they don't fathom ; but for his great heart.
They feel him : he feels them.   All men he wins,
Through that electric potency which leaps
When a great intellect is fired by soul.

QUEEN.

My faithful Montmorin, this puissant voice,
Hath it then tuned thy heart to beat
To the false music of a demagogue ?
What says La Mark ?   If thou, too, yieldest thee,
The citadel itself, — its outworks seized, —
Must yield.

LA MARK.

You've seen a tall, stout edifice
Enwrapt in flames, their eager, sharpened tongues
Snatching and biting what they can lay hold of;
And, — all consumed that was combustible, —
You've seen the walls erect, and the pile's core,
The heat-dispensing chimney, undevoured,
Uninjured, steadfast, ready for new service.
Such is Count Mirabeau, a prey to passions
Which raged about his soul, but could not waste it.
To tyranny, too, a prey.   In his hot youth,
Boiling with life, bounding with action's zest,
By a stern father's rigor he was thrust

In dungeon after dungeon, sunniest years
Of a rich manhood's prime darkly engulfed
In the unmanning solitude of prisons, —
Imprisonment unearned, harsh at the best,
Tow'rds him cruel, undue.   That his young heart
Came thence unshriveled ; nay, that he did seem
To thrive on what had quenched a lesser man,
His great soul swelling 'gainst oppression's grip,
Proves what victorious mettle hives in him.
He stands alone, majestic by ascent,
A giant, with will to do a savior's work.
I pray your Majesty to pardon me :
I speak with warmth because I know this man.

QUEEN.

Friendship diverteth opportunities.
'Tis right that love should candy o'er defects.
Noble Malherbes, a great high magistrate
Should be a judge of men.   Say frankly now,
What is Count Mirabeau ?

MALHERBES.

     A man to be won
For a good cause, not for a bad one, Madame.

QUEEN.

Ha !   From you that is robust eulogy.

MALHERBES.

Your Majesty, our human elements,
Distensive, fine, illimitable in themselves,
Are by such subtle hand commingled deep,
That in a many-sided concrete form,
Sparkling with mind's rebound, burnished by soul,
An individual man, had he less reach,
And recesses lurking less deep than this,
Baffles the shrewdest insight, baffles it
With the mysteriousness of his resource.
Yet still, methinks, that through the dazzlement,
The eclipsing coruscations of his genius,
I can descry the bent of Mirabeau.
I've watched him playing at the social board,
I've heard him roaring from his lair, the tribune,
I've seen the lion shake his bristled mane,
And smiled and joyed to witness how the wolves,
Foxes, hyenas, all the baser breeds,
Shrank trembling into their small envious selves ;
And even the nobler tribes admired with awe.

QUEEN.

Much cause have I to dread that fiery voice.

MALHERBES.

Madame, Count Mirabeau, with other men,
Some of the best, many of his own order,

Think this great earthquake's rumble could not be
So universal, and continuous loud,
But for supernal sanction, whose deep aim
It is, hereby to aver the aching wrongs
The multitudinous people have groaned under
So long, so patiently.   To the world's end
Count Mirabeau's far trumpet voice
Hath sounded these wide wrongs, whose swift redress
Is the first duty of the burdened hour.
Redress, he thinks, will the most safely come
And surely, through the King's co-agency.
But many think, with him, — your pardon, count, —
                                    [*To* MONTMORIN.
The present ministry lack forecast, vigor.

QUEEN.

Vigor he has, with intellect's far range
And clasp ; but has he moral weight and will ?

MALHERBES.

The will he has, and he can give it weight.
A sapful, large, aspiring nature needs,
To be itself, room for its amplitude.
Crossed, tethered, it will gore itself and others,
From panting restlessness of devious growth.

Enter the DAUPHIN *(about six years old).*

DAUPHIN.

Dear mamma, General La Fayette is coming.

QUEEN.

Go thou and bring him in.

DAUPHIN.

No : I don't like him.

KING.

What is this ? Who has taught thee so foolishly ?

DAUPHIN.

Your Majesty, 'tis I have taught myself.

Enter a CHAMBERLAIN.

CHAMBERLAIN.

Your Majesties, the General La Fayette.

Enter LA FAYETTE.

KING.

General, I hope you bring us no bad news :
Paris is quiet ?

LA FAYETTE.

Sire, as quiet as
Can be a boiling caldron.

QUEEN.

What doth feed
The flames that keep the caldron boiling on?

LA FAYETTE.

Your Majesty, hunger is their chief feeder.

DAUPHIN.

Monsieur de La Fayette, it seems to me
That you are more the King than is papa.

LA FAYETTE.

Your Highness, I have come to-day to know
The King's commands in an important business.

QUEEN.

Sire, we will leave you to this conference.

[*Exeunt* QUEEN, DAUPHIN, MONTMORIN, MALHERBES,
and LA MARK

The Scene closes.

SCENE III.

Cecile's Apartment.

CECILE (*alone ; in deep mourning*).

Blest spirits, bless me, before my time,
   With sprinklings of celestial dew,
   That my touched eyes, beholding you,
Forefeel their bliss of rights sublime.

Thou heavenly guest, my Henri gone,
   Let me, O let me look on thee,
   As thou canst look, and dost, on me ;
And then I shall not be alone.

I hear, I hear them whispering soft :
   O how it glads my widowed heart.
   My Henri's, his I hear apart,
Sweetening their harmonies aloft ;

A voice, whose music is a chain
   Enlinkt with thoughts my dearest, best ;
   Reviving echo, in my breast,
Sonorous through my thankful brain.

5

I hear it now : no more I'll moan :
    I'll warm me with its sacred sound :
    I know that thee I have refound.
I'll weep no more : I'm not alone.

Enter a SERVANT *and gives her a card.*

CECILE.

Is he below?

SERVANT.

    Madame, he is ; and says,
His business is of present need.

CECILE.

    Admit him.

Enter MIRABEAU.

MIRABEAU.

Madame, from an old friend in Languedoc
Is come to me a package, with appeal
That to yourself, and to no other hand,
It be delivered on the instant's spur.
'Tis from the Sieur Martin.

CECILE.

    The Sieur Martin!
Our dear, dear friend.   You bring, Count Mirabeau,

A treasure to me, letters from my husband
To Sieur Martin, letters his last.   I thank you.

As Mirabeau *approaches nearer to give her the package, he
partly recognizes her.*

MIRABEAU.

Your countenance, lady, is not strange to me.

CECILE.

'Tis my high fortune, Count, to meet you twice,
Each time as benefactor.   Twelve months since
You helped to wrest me from ferocious claws.

MIRABEAU.

Well I remember.   Yours is not a face
Whose impress passes.   To be beautiful —
What privileges wait on that high presence !
Warm beauty is a daily Sun : its beam
Delight and love, fertility and life
Drink up with greed.   'Tis woman's gorgeous might,
Her sceptre's flash, wherewith she sways the world ;
But as her kingdom is man's heart, her best,
Her broadest power is beauty's smile.   When lips
Smile with the fervent eye in liveliest league,
You swear us servants to your utmost will.
Dear lady, do not frown.

CECILE.

I do not frown.

Should I not smile with pride, Count Mirabeau,
At th' honor you do me, making my floor
Your study for rhetorical rehearsal
And multiplying me into an audience —

MIRABEAU.

Me and yourself you wrong.   I never feign :
Phrasemonger I can't be.   Heart prompts the head
With me.   And for yourself, you are too coy,
Too unapprised, to feel by quick rebound
How sudden strong the coils may be you cast
Unconsciously upon a manly heart.
I swear to you —

CECILE.

Count Mirabeau, swear not.

MIRABEAU.

You would rebuke, repel me —

CECILE.

Nay, not so.

I would remind you of yourself.

MIRABEAU.

Myself

Am now your slave.

CECILE.

I'll have no slave : no, none.

Least would I have Count Mirabeau my slave.
Himself I'd have him be, and that he's not
When he lets passion, — as he were a boy, —
Entwine about and fling him to the ground,
There to be grimed with appetite's excess ;
While his great powers stand locked in silent shame,
To see a mightiness shrunk to the mood
Of vulgarest feeders.

MIRABEAU.

Heavens !   Thou echoest me

When my best thoughts are uppermost.

CECILE.

Let them

Ever be uppermost.   This beauty's sway
Which thou didst speak of — thou hast seized but half,
The nether half, of its creativeness.
Beauty is the earth's light, lighting to Heaven !
Out of all thought, all act, all life there shoots
Upward a spirit seeking for betterment.
Of being's breath this is the vital virtue.
Than sensuous beauty's sheen far fairer this,
Far potenter, mounting on aspiration :
Men who aspire not are scarce more than beasts.

MIRABEAU.

Thou joy'st my brain with a new fervor's birth.

CECILE.

A shimmering phantom this to most men seems,
A vision not believed in, caught by few,
And semblable to air.   But wouldst thou seize
This phantom, closely hug it to thy breast,
Embrace it with thy warmest, deepest breath,
'Twould graft into thy blood a sap whose flow
Would sweeten every thought, and swell thy brain
Daily to bloom with truth, with duty's life.

MIRABEAU.

Thou speak'st a tongue I never heard till now.

CECILE.

Thyself dost prompt my speech.   There is a light
Within thee thou'st not given full air to yet ;
A height higher than thou canst know of, till
Inward illuminant unseals a world.
There is a conquest thou couldst win, to which
Thy boldest triumphs in the tribune are
The transient tremors of an earthquake's shock
To the eternal victory of the Sun.
To swing thee up to this new loftiness,
Where the whole world shall wonder at thee, not

As now with dread or doubt, but joy and worship,
For this, purge thee of transitory loves,
Unsmother the divine that's pent in thee.
I do but read thy possibilities.

MIRABEAU.

My guardian angel thou !

CECILE.

A guardian angel
Hast thou whose guardianship to the keen edge
Is whetted which only that love can take
Whose warm nest is a mother's patient heart.
Her smile was the loved plaything of thy cradle,
Her tears were prayers to ease thy sorrow's sting,
And her affections swathed thee in their life
Through the rude buffets of thy manhood's war.
And now that guardianship consummate is
In the celestial liberty of flight ;
Now thoughts and wishes are themselves their wings
To speed them to their aim, their aim being thee.
To be with thee, this is her angelhood,
Which hath its chilly shadows when thou stoop'st
To smirch thee in the earth's uncleanliness.
For now her being is entwined with thine,
As when she bore thee 'neath her hopeful breast.
Thou canst not speak or do but she is privy,

A watchful angel ever hovering near thee.
Hark to her heavenly rustle, joyful whisper:
She pours her mother's blessing on thee.

> MIRABEAU *bends half kneeling.* CECILE *stretches out both hands over him, her head and eyes turned upward.*

> *The Curtain falls.*

ACT III.

SCENE I.

Mirabeau's Apartment.

MIRABEAU (*alone*).

THEY chafe me with their dull delays, their deadness;
And most of all, their ignorant mistrust.
To the shook sides of a volcano clings
The court.   It rumbles, smokes, by night at times
It belches flame ; and they've nor power to quench
Nor will to spring away.   O I could save them,
And saving them, save France, would they but so.
Within me this brave epoch's soul I feel,
As in my marrow had been hotly pouring
For forty years the lava of the times.
Two cubs were we, I and young Revolution ;
I've sucked at the same dugs with so much breath,
Growing its growth and strengthening with its strength,
That now I'm kindred stout enough to be
The monster's favorite keeper, and to sit
Between his horns and guide him. — Ha ! myself
Am muzzled, guarded, gyved, as though I were
A dangerous beast.   O I could rush away,

To still the throbbings of my heated heart
In the wide silence of some trackless waste.
They'll not be stilled : for man is made to mount ;
And I could, mounting, carry on my shoulders,
Lifted to ample planes, my fellow-men.
What rapture to repeat the Cardinal's boast :
" Under my prescient watch France sleeps secure."

Enter LA MARK.

LA MARK.

The General La Fayette is close behind me.

MIRABEAU.

'Twill be of no avail.   How can I yoke
With such a pullback ?   My dear Count, this man
Is a rank solecism, medley perverse :
Ambitious sentimentalist he is,
Grandison-Cromwell.

LA MARK.

              Yourself did prompt the meeting ;
The King and Queen, they cheer it with their hope.

MIRABEAU.

What can come of 't?   I see things as they are.
Corruption, want, and fear make of this land
A maskèd hell, where every man is loosed

Upon himself, and where there is no God.
This chaos, — come of misrule's arrogance,
Whose fruit is cruelty and wrong and vice, —
Gives life to untruth, glib duplicities,
Laying arenas where the selfish false
Will triumphs howl, like tigers in the lists.
Throw out a cork to sound the ocean's depth :
Catch loudest cannon's freight with fisher's net :
As well do this as hope through La Fayette
To rule this frantic revolution's rage.

LA MARK.

Dear Count, this is no statesman's mood you're in.
I'll meet him at the threshold, say you're ill ;
For that you surely are.

MIRABEAU.
                    O pardon me.
I'm always ill, of false defeats and routs
Which should be victories.   But now I'm well ;
Let La Fayette come in, I will be meek :
I will be humble.

ATTENDANT *entering, announces* GENERAL LA FAYETTE.

Enter LA FAYETTE.

MIRABEAU.

General, with frank intent I meet you here,

And with a heart bounding with hoarded wishes
For such fair issue to this conference
That it to both shall be a joy forever.

LA FAYETTE.

Count Mirabeau, your generous sentiments
I give you back from a full heart.   We two
Might work some good together.

MIRABEAU.

                       Some ! great good,
A good immeasurable.   Chief want of France,
Her want of wants, is an executive.
We have a King, a King newly empowered,
And full empowered.   But he is held in leash
By the Assembly, by yourself, by Paris.

LA FAYETTE.

Th' Assembly has, by solemnized decree,
Given to the King all execution's rights.
In the wild turmoil of destructive change,
And the new jealousy of royal sway,
'Tis found expedient, for the King's own safety,
To check this sway of widest total swing.
This is but transitory, a protection,
Thin barrier for our present good and his.

Sound ministers, and other legal tools,
He has for constitutional command.

MIRABEAU.

This your protection is from day to day
Bringing him into more and more contempt.
For man or King contempt is deadliest blast.
A King who is protected is no King.
'Tis thus that Kings are marshaled to the block.
Necker, his present first adviser, is
As fit to guide the currents of a state,
Rocked by this earthquake heave of revolution,
As I to hush the whirlwind's roar.   General,
Let us be frank.   The two chief powers in France
Are you and I.   Let us unite, to bless,
To rescue France.   Your lofty qualities
Need my impulsion to empower them,
And my impulsion needs your qualities
To temper it, and gain it deference.

LA FAYETTE.

Were I to move more swiftly, in a trice
The slippery ground would trip me to a fall.

MIRABEAU.

This is no time to lead by following.

LA FAYETTE.

To keep command there must be something yielded.

MIRABEAU.

There must be ever new initiatives
In him who'd keep command.   Courage and bold-
ness
Should aye go hand in hand.   The courage, Marquis,
You have : boldness you lack.

LA FAYETTE.

                              Who can outdare
The madness of these times?

MIRABEAU.

                              Their madness 'tis
That needs the stoutest will.   Never was age
When for the loftiest leadership there was
A warmer urgency.   Wolves in fierce herds
Grow daily fiercer, hungrier, bolder, bloodier.
Be they not mastered, on themselves they'll prey,
Then call in tigers to advise them.   'No time this
To wait upon events.   'Tis just the time
To seize'events, quick moulding them anew,
Crushing the chaos out of them, and thus
With foresight make their lowering darkness yield
Sparkles and beams to be by wisdom wrought

To calm and wide illumination's cheer.
In blackest, gloomiest epochs shines a light
Can lead them, shines in his mind who espies
Their causes, tendencies, and certain scope.
All opposition yields to mental might.
Power obeys and hath a joy in power.
The tempest drowns in rage the weaker ship;
But with the strong, that boldly braves its worst,
It plays, and then, subsiding from its wrath,
With sunshine flatters it.

LA FAYETTE.

           Count Mirabeau,
From mine your view of things differs so much,
I see not how we could just now co-work.
Perhaps a little later —

MIRABEAU.

           A little later!
And still another little later, and
You'll find you in a lateness, where the wreck, —
And such a wreck! — is all that eyes will see,
Eyes that have been convulsed by horrors' glare,
Horrors not dreamt of now, save in the hearts
(If demons' breasts hold hearts) where their black
       brood

Is just beginning to be hatched in thoughts
That at the first make e'en their breeders pale.

LA FAYETTE.

I cannot grasp such dark imaginings.
Permit me, gentlemen, to take my leave.

[*Exit.*

MIRABEAU.

And this man sways the fate of France to-day !
A man to whom the play of circumstances,
Mysterious play, hath given, o'er the vast future,
Present control, — the dumb, deep-thoughted future ;
And he can't peer beyond to-morrow's rim :
A man who at a time like this, — a time
When every pulse this troubled nation throbs
Is parent of great consequences, — rules
From hand to mouth, a passive leader, and,
Lapt in the vanities of hope, believes,
Because he's tossed on the loose, washy froth
Of temporary popularity,
That he's a power, a power permanent,
All capable to govern such a storm ;
As though the crests that momentary glisten
On dark, tempestuous billows, swayed their motion.

LA MARK.

I feared this issue.   La Fayette will not

Play second part, cannot play first ; and so
We drift each week, each day, nearer to ruin.

MIRABEAU.

He did good service in America,
Under the mighty wing of Washington ;
And thence the blunder that himself has pinion
For a far, towering, national flight in France.
Without one greatness of that glorious man,
He'd like to be a Washington for us.
These giants never are repeated, nor
Can small men mimic their majestic gait.
The General La Fayette has culminated.
More dangerous grows the slippery ground he fears.
Nothing has he but popularity,
A reed shook by the breath of fickle men ;
No reason's sweep beyond the present's maze,
No vision of the possibilities.
The Court distrusts him, and it shall do more. —
But reads the Court my notes ? or, reading them,
Gives to them any heed ?   O could they see
As I see, they'd redeem themselves and France.
What I could do for them, and my dear France,
Would lift my name beside great Washington's.
Purely and nobly did he move and rule
In his vast sphere ; and rich, he still was paid :
All public servants should be, large and small.

6

Yet Calumny would plant its fangs in me.
As penny to a million pounds, is what
The King pays me, to what I'll do for him,
If he will let me.   Will he not — my friend,
The populace will cuff their bleeding corpses.

LA MARK.

Great God !   You frighten me !

MIRABEAU.

          'Tis true, 'tis true:
But still I'll not despair, I'll not despair.
While I have life and faculties, I'll work.
Now to the Assembly.

LA MARK.

        I'll be there anon.

                [*Exeunt severally.*

SCENE II.

Garden of St. Cloud.

Enter a lady of the QUEEN'S *household, who admits* MIRABEAU
through a portal visible from the stage ; then exit.

MIRABEAU (*alone*).

Powers invisible, who hold the singled threads
Whereof is daily spun our mystic life,
If e'er you favored me, favor me now :
Upon this interview great issues hang.

Enter the QUEEN.

QUEEN.

Count Mirabeau, by your entreaty pressed,
I meet you.   The resolve this to concede
Had in it less of hope than of despair.

MIRABEAU.

Most gracious Madame, speak not of despair :
The refuge of the wicked is despair.
Think me not bold or vauntful, but to me
Grant a full faith, alliance cordial, and
I pledge my head, all that I am or can be,
The Sun of hope shall swiftly reascend
To his lost zenith.

QUEEN.

Where he has not been
These many, many months.　He's near his setting,
Behind such clouds, black, ominous, that I
And mine feel gathering close a curtain's folds
No morn will ever lift.　Long have I been
The mark of hates, of hates strange and perverse.
Yourself have hated me.

MIRABEAU.

Never, O never !
No, personally never, nor e'en regally.
The Revolution aimed, not at the King,
But at th' abuses of authority.
I led the Revolution : 'twas my part,
And still I'll lead and rule it.　Royalty
Is now renewed, shorn of Cæsarian ills.
France undergoes regeneration's bath.
Her safety lies in monarchy reformed.
For a Republic's reach she's yet too green.
To save the monarchy is to save France.
And what a service !　What a regal task !
We can achieve this task, yes, you and I.
Repel me not ; no more suspect me ; trust me.
My life to-day is fresh with aspiration.
I, too, I am regenerate.　I am
Not what I have been.　Men who do not grow

Are worthless for the great occasions.   Me
The fates have tried, how deeply none can know
But th' innocent, whose being has been gnawed
By chains for years in silent dungeon's desert.
My passions, the hot life within me, saved me:
They bore me onward, upward.   None but men
Passion-empowered quicken into greatness.
Horizons widen as I mount the years.
O Madame, gracious Queen, mistrust me not.

QUEEN.

Your mien, your looks, your speech, are of a man
Who has a soul, a true, deep, generous soul.
Count Mirabeau — yes, yes, I trust you.

MIRABEAU.

O !

This is the greatest day I've lived — a day
Shall be the parent of still greater days.

QUEEN.

Be not too confident.   Your ally's wounded,
Struck by the poisoned shafts of Calumny.
No air that I can breathe but it is fouled
By slanders, hissed from the gross guilty throats
Of kings, of populace, of cardinals,
Of nobles, gentry, rabble, citizens,

Of men and women.   Children even are taught
To turn their pretty looks from me, as one
Would taint their innocence.   The cynosure
Am I of universal hate ; as though
Mysterious Providence had chosen me
To be a sacrificial·offering
To all humanity for the deep sins
Of foregone kings and queens against mankind.

MIRABEAU.

Most royal lady, every word you speak
Kindles my courage, braces my resolves.

QUEEN.

And your brave speech would warm my confidence,
Were 't not so inly chilled by suffering.
At my sad birthday was I marked for woe.
Convulsion was my midwife : I was born
The day that Lisbon was by earthquake whelmed ;
And ever since the ground shakes under me.
Portents malign have dogged my track, to point
Their skeleton fingers towards some hoarded curse.

MIRABEAU.

Your cause should summon a new chivalry,
And fire all noble manhood to your side.

QUEEN.

The times are shrunk from ancient nobleness.
Envy and jealousy usurp all hearts.
My natural defenders are my worst foes.

MIRABEAU.

O, France is not entombed in infamy :
There is a manhood can be roused and shall be,
Within the abounding confines of this land,
Shall rescue you from base imprisonment
To this perverted, unslaked populace,
Played on by weak ambition's policy.
This scheme of rescue, born within my heart,
Is ripening in my brain, and its success
Shall save us all from brutal anarchy.
Courage, most noble Queen : this hour is big
With great salvations.

QUEEN.

    For my children's sake
And the poor King, I will catch solacement
From your bold promises.   A mother's pangs
Of daily fear for her loved offspring's perils,
Are sharpened for a Queen with double edge.
On me let man's and Heaven's will be done ;
But save my children.

MIRABEAU.

What I have or can,
My power, will, life, I pledge to you, great Queen.
All of myself I dedicate to you.

QUEEN.

My thanks, a mother's thanks, a Queen's I give you.
And all I can of aid I'll lend you.

[*She holds out her hand for him to kiss.*

MIRABEAU.

On my knee
I swear, if but my life.be spared, I'll save you.

The Curtain drops.

SCENE III.

A Street in Paris : a crowd of Laborers and Women.

FIRST LABORER.

What has the Assembly done for us ?

SECOND LABORER.

Bread is dearer, work no better paid, and less of it.

THIRD LABORER.

The rich are more selfish than ever, spend more

on themselves : and yet fewer francs come into our pockets.

FIRST LABORER.

Each member of the Assembly gets eighteen francs a day, the most of them for doing nothing, and I can earn but a franc a day when I have work, and when I do nothing I get nothing.

SECOND LABORER.

This is the hardest winter I ever knew, and the summer promises no better.   What shall we do?

THIRD LABORER.

Here comes Couthon ; he always has a word for the poor.

Enter COUTHON.

Tell us, Citizen Couthon, when will bread be cheaper?

COUTHON.

Not till the people take things into their own hands.

FIRST LABORER.

This Assembly does nothing for Paris.

COUTHON.

No, and they never will till they are forced.   Their interest it is to sit and sit forever, and do nothing, so long as they are well paid for it.

SECOND LABORER.

It's very hard that there should be so many rich men who eat meat and drink wine every day and do no work, while we who work from sunrise to sunset can barely earn bread enough to keep us from starving.

A WOMAN.

My children have had but half allowance for weeks.

COUTHON.

No man should be rich while his neighbors are poor. What's the Revolution for, if men are not to be made equal?

Enter at the side, without being at first perceived by the crowd, MIRABEAU, *pale, leaning on the arm of his secretary,* PELLENC.

MIRABEAU.

Is not this field of rich humanity
To be deep ploughed by new desires, new wants,
New hopes, and thus reveal new roots, new seeds,
To bear new fruit through far eternity?
Nature commands that we go onward, upward.
Think you you can bid nature warp her track,
And lift blind, groping evil sovereign —
Evil, which is life's sickness, life's wan jailer?
To stop, to pause, were to begin to sink
Towards rottenness, which is but rankest evil.

When we cease going forward, we go backward.
How shallowly men strive to heal life's ills.
Each has his puny cure, drawn mostly from
A muddy pond of petted egotism.
He thinks he seeks the truth ; he seeks himself.
Each one is armed with crude imaginations,
Wherewith he would besiege and mine the truth,
Which is, to assail a barbacan with clouds;
For, competent imaginations can
Shoot but from natures rich and arable.
But truth they hide for ages with their fog.
How few are they can grasp great principles.
Most people see but with their belly's eyes ;
And empty bellies blind the other senses.
Some see but with the bloodshot glance of war ;
Some with ambition's feverish, fretful looks ;
And this has been one of my weaknesses.
To range through the clear spaces where clean truth
Smiles lustrous with a showering radiancy,
Aspiring thought should bear no weight of self.
Let us go in, Pellenc : I'm weak to-day.

SEVERAL LABORERS.

Vive Mirabeau ! Vive Mirabeau !

FIRST LABORER.

Count Mirabeau, why does not the Assembly do
something for the people ?

SECOND LABORER.

We are willing to work, and can get no work. Can't
they give us work and better wages?

THIRD LABORER.

They talk and talk, while we starve.

MIRABEAU.

You are a mason ; can you build a house
From base to cornice in a week, a month ?
And what if first you must pull down an old one?
Never by Legislature was a work,
A deeper, larger, done in shorter time
Than by this French Assembly.   My good friends,
In public as in private things, he who
Lacks patience, loses something of his life.
Know you what this Assembly is ?   It is
An overtopping rival of the King,
The Church, the haughty aristocracy,
Single, sudden, triumphant conqueror
Of rooted despotisms, that have grieved, wronged,
And scourged this plundered land for centuries.
Sprung from the people's bosom, it hath struck
A triple tyranny with dread and awe,
Wrenched from incestuous couch close-linkèd sways,
And to th' enfranchised ground dashed them all
          shivered ;

Set thought so free, that through the hoary darkness
A thousand flames now lighten from the earth
To marry joyful flashes poured from heaven.
Pardon me : I can speak no more to-day,
I'm ill ; I fear me very ill.

> [*Exit with* Pellenc.

MANY VOICES.

Vive Mirabeau !

COUTHON.

Why do you beshout this royalist, this arch aristo-
crat ?

FIRST LABORER.

Couthon, whatever else he be, he loves the people ;
he has a soul, this man, to love all men.   Vive Mirabeau !

> *The crowd joins in the shout, and the scene closes.*

SCENE IV.

Vestibule of the Assembly.

Enter two MEMBERS, *meeting.*

FIRST MEMBER.

Does Mirabeau make his speech on Wills to-day ?

SECOND MEMBER.

I've come to hear it.   Is he in his seat ?

FIRST MEMBER.

Not yet.   The subject is not one for him to shine in.

SECOND MEMBER.

If he puts himself into it he can make a cold subject glow, a dry one sparkle.   'Tis late for him.

Enter THIRD MEMBER.

THIRD MEMBER.

Have you heard the news ?   Mirabeau is ill, very ill.

SECOND MEMBER.

Not dangerously ?

THIRD MEMBER.

I fear so.   Cabanis, his physician, I saw just now.
He is uneasy, looked grave.

SECOND MEMBER.

Great God !   Were Mirabeau to die !

FIRST MEMBER.

I have not so much trust in him as you have ; but
his death were a calamity to France.

SECOND MEMBER.

A calamity incommensurable, irreparable. Let us go to his house and make inquiry. His death would shake all France, and in the Assembly leave a void — nay, it would change the very nature of our body.

[*Exeunt.*

SCENE V.

The Street, before Mirabeau's House.

Enter from both sides a number of people of different ranks.

FIRST CITIZEN (*to* SECOND).

Is it true that Mirabeau is ill ?

SECOND CITIZEN.

So I heard at the other side of the city, and hastened hither to know.

[*To* THIRD CITIZEN.

Is his attack dangerous ?

THIRD CITIZEN.

I hear it is. France could better lose a score of her best citizens and statesmen than this one Mirabeau.

Enter the two MEMBERS OF THE ASSEMBLY.

SECOND MEMBER (*to* THIRD CITIZEN).

What is the last report ?

THIRD CITIZEN.

That he is very ill.   Here is Robespierre : he may
have the latest.

Enter ROBESPIERRE.

Citizen Robespierre, what is his condition ?

ROBESPIERRE.

I heard but now of his illness, and am come to
learn his state.

[*Aside.*

Aye, Maximilian Robespierre, thou wouldst be
A greater man were Mirabeau away.
He shrivels all ambitions save his own.
Here's one with liveliest joy in his black heart,
That scoundrel wretch, Marat.

Enter MARAT.

MARAT (*aside*).

                    Ha ! Robespierre !
The cowardly hypocrite !   What does he here ?
I'm here to learn good news.

[*To a* CITIZEN.

How is he now ?

CITIZEN.

The last of many rumors is, he's better.

MARAT (*aside*).

That's bad news for Marat.   But still there's hope.

[*To a* CITIZEN *just entered.*

Canst tell how goes it now with Mirabeau ?

CITIZEN.

'Tis said he's sinking fast.

MARAT (*aside*).

Ha ! Let him sink !

As he doth sink, Marat and others rise.

SECOND MEMBER

O one more year of life for Mirabeau !
His death were now a great catastrophe
In this most terrible of tragedies
We are enacting, and would hasten greater.

The Scene closes.

SCENE VI.

Death-bed of Mirabeau.

MIRABEAU, LA MARK, CABANIS, FROCHON, PELLENC.

MIRABEAU (*on a couch*).

My dear La Mark, thou who on battle-fields
Hast seen so many die heroic deaths,

7

Art thou content with me?—Only afar,
When in life's lusty heat we think of him,
Seems death a frowning foe.   In the full throb
Of enterprise and action, his stark image
Maims the hot haste of eager, manful blood,.—
A momentary threat, and discord rude.
But when the pulse beats languidly, and brain,
Wan with the loss of fleet phosphoric flood,
Is pale and passive, then he smiles a friend,
Who comes armed for our rescue.   Cabanis,
Is it not so?

CABANIS.

   To all her precious children
Nature is kind ; and when their time is come
That they return unto their mother's bosom,
She soothes their senses for the mortal change.

LA MARK.

At the great hour of death are nearer us
Beings unseen, whose quick affinities
Are part and tissue of our earthly life ;
And, for the worldly shocks of conflict coarse
They bring the soft embrace of harmonies,
So lapping us in influence Elysian,
The chastened spirit passes on in peace.

     MIRABEAU *presses* LA MARK'S *hand.*

Enter his VALET.

MIRABEAU.

What is it, Louis?

VALET.

Sir, a messenger
From the Assembly.

MIRABEAU.

Kind Pellenc, receive him.

[*Exit* PELLENC, *who soon returns.*

PELLENC.

The Assembly to Count Mirabeau send greeting,
With earnest wishes and warm sympathy.

MIRABEAU.

Thanks, thanks.	Answer with cordial thanks and
    love.
[*Exit* PELLENC.

The voice of Mirabeau they'll hear no more;
And some, aye, many, will regret that voice.
There were things yet to say and do. — 'Tis past.

Reënter PELLENC.

PELLENC.

For the Ambassadors their envoy speaks
Best wishes and respectful salutation.

MIRABEAU.

For their considerate courtesy I send
Grateful acknowledgment.

[*Exit* PELLENC.

What Mirabeau
Will do or counsel will no more confound them,
Yet they'll be puzzled more without than with him.

Reënter PELLENC *with* MONTMORIN.

MONTMORIN.

The King and Queen wait anxious my return.

MIRABEAU.

Speak my most loving duty and my thanks.
O! Montmorin, now I too mourn my going.
Plans, purposes, and will, all ripe to save them.
This head, this head: could it be left behind
For the poor Queen! — Ha! Horror! horror! horror!
See there! See there! It rains blood-drops, pure
          blood!
I see it on your faces! Horrible! Horrible!
Look, look! It curls up from the wetted ground
In mist of flame, as from a reddening hell!
Ha! See those demons dancing through the flames,
Lapping the bloody drops fast as they fall.
And now they put on human features' likeness!

More like, more like they grow !   Horror of horrors !
Faces I know !   O God ! O God !

> [*Falls back in* LA MARK'S *arms.*

> *The Scene closes.*

SCENE VII.

The same as Scene V.   Street before Mirabeau's House.

People coming and going with anxious looks. FIRST *and* SECOND
MEMBERS OF THE ASSEMBLY, ROBESPIERRE, *and* MARAT *as
before.*

SECOND MEMBER.

Paris and France hold in their frightened breath,
While whispers fill the sky with bootless prayer.
For this great death big tears will drown the land.
When he is gone History will shift her course :
One of her channels flowed swift through his brain.

ROBESPIERRE (*aside*).

Already is the air lighter to breathe,
Enlarged is Robespierre ; for, strong Mirabeau
Kept him imprisoned.   Back, back to my brain,
Dear thoughts, lest ye betray me through my eyes.
Men must not see my joy upon my face.

MARAT (*aside*).

He was a rock ever in front of us,
Threatening destruction.   Giant he was, this man,
With might to uphold a tottering monarchy.
Down it now goes, and with it all that lifts
The arrogant and rich above their fellows.

SCENE VIII.

A room in the Palace of the Tuileries.

The KING, *the* QUEEN, MALHERBES, MINISTERS, MEMBERS OF
THE COURT.   *To them enter* MONTMORIN.

MONTMORIN.

Neither better nor worse.   Whilst I was there
He fainted, but he soon revived, then slept.
Cabanis will not speak ; he looks his fears.
                          [*They whisper among themselves.*

Enter LA MARK.

LA MARK.

A void, an aching void, in every heart.
Paris is empty !   France is empty !

MONTMORIN.

Ha !

Here is La Mark.   He brings the latest news.
Is there a hope ?

LA MARK.

Hope !   Mirabeau is dead !

The QUEEN *shrieks and falls on a sofa, and the curtain*
                                                    drops.